God Loves You –
Joy M Nall

The Candy Cane Story

A Christian Story

by Joy Merchant Nall and Thomas Nall, Jr.

Dedicated to our Children:
Jessica & Kylie Nall and Spencer & Aaron Gillette

illustrated by
Amy Floyd Gillette

Long, Long ago there was a candymaker
named Mr. Sugarbaker who had a wonderful
candy store and workshop with his sweet wife,
Mrs. Sugarbaker. Now, Mr. Sugarbaker worked
happily every day making his usual goodies,
but he was most famous for all of his
new candy creations.

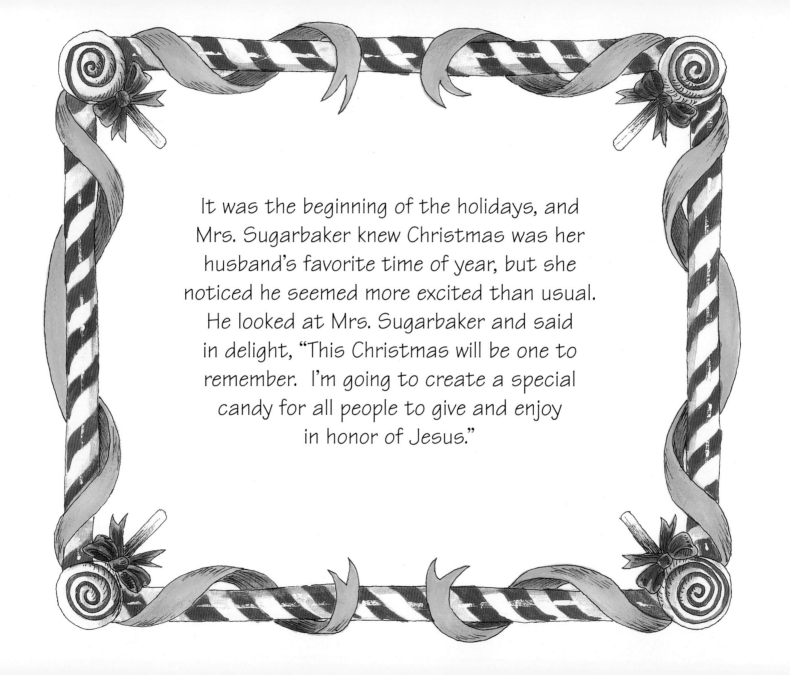

It was the beginning of the holidays, and Mrs. Sugarbaker knew Christmas was her husband's favorite time of year, but she noticed he seemed more excited than usual. He looked at Mrs. Sugarbaker and said in delight, "This Christmas will be one to remember. I'm going to create a special candy for all people to give and enjoy in honor of Jesus."

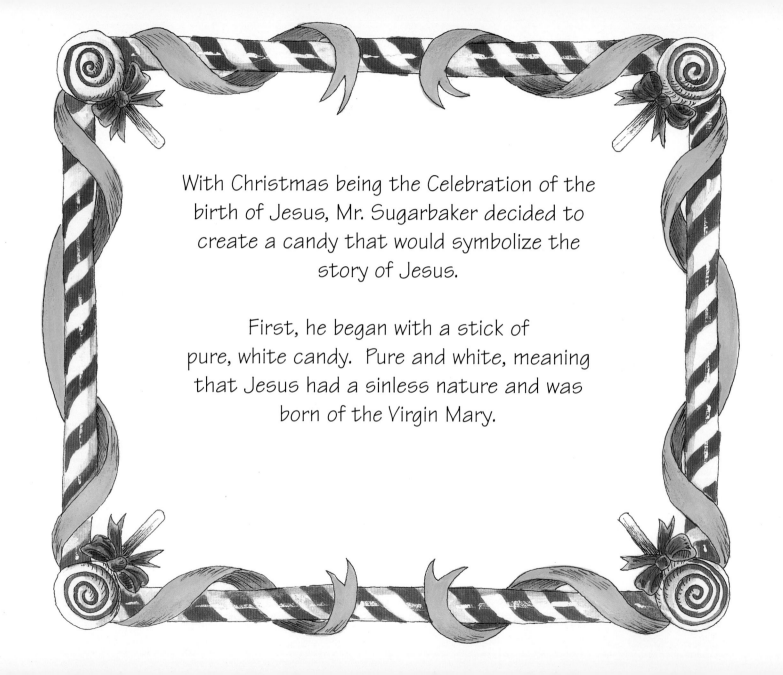

With Christmas being the Celebration of the birth of Jesus, Mr. Sugarbaker decided to create a candy that would symbolize the story of Jesus.

First, he began with a stick of pure, white candy. Pure and white, meaning that Jesus had a sinless nature and was born of the Virgin Mary.

Next, Mr. Sugarbaker needed to shape his candy. His wife, being quite the helper, said, "May I suggest the letter J, the first letter from the beautiful name of Jesus." "What a great idea," he replied. They grinned at one another as he started to bend the candy.

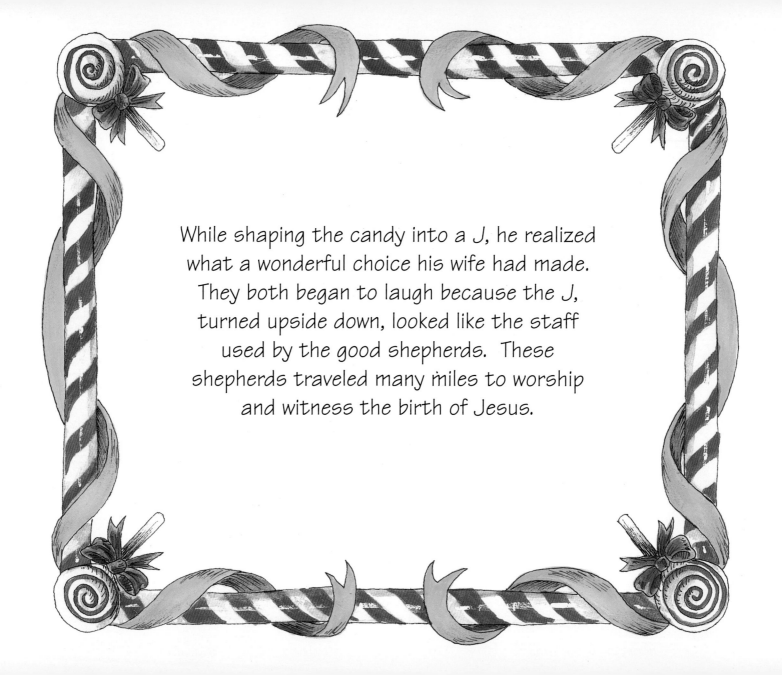

While shaping the candy into a J, he realized
what a wonderful choice his wife had made.
They both began to laugh because the J,
turned upside down, looked like the staff
used by the good shepherds. These
shepherds traveled many miles to worship
and witness the birth of Jesus.

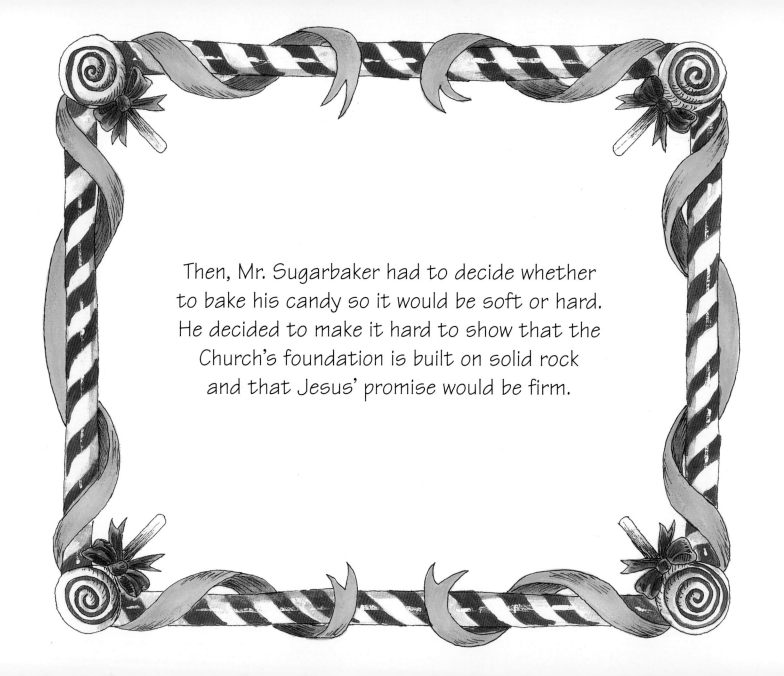

Then, Mr. Sugarbaker had to decide whether
to bake his candy so it would be soft or hard.
He decided to make it hard to show that the
Church's foundation is built on solid rock
and that Jesus' promise would be firm.

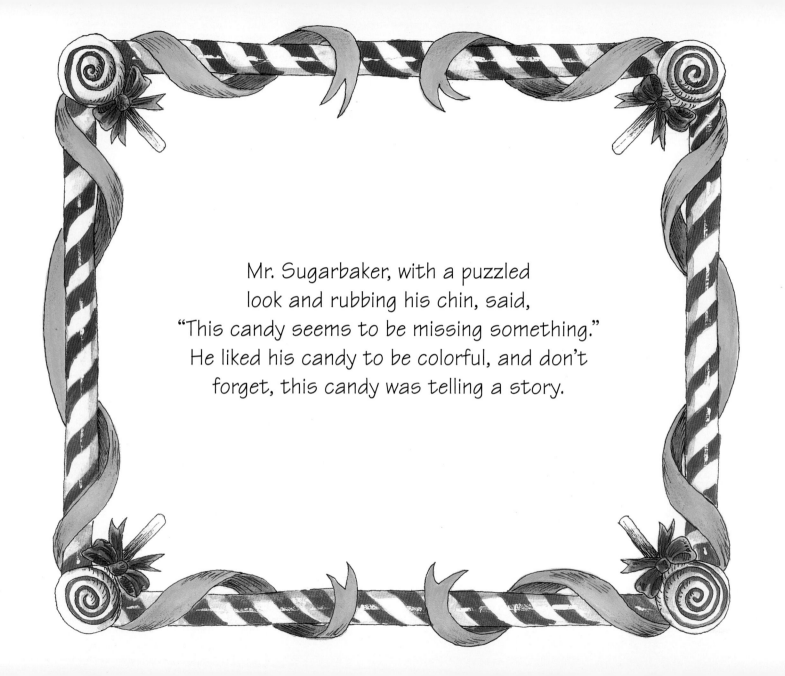

Mr. Sugarbaker, with a puzzled
look and rubbing his chin, said,
"This candy seems to be missing something."
He liked his candy to be colorful, and don't
forget, this candy was telling a story.

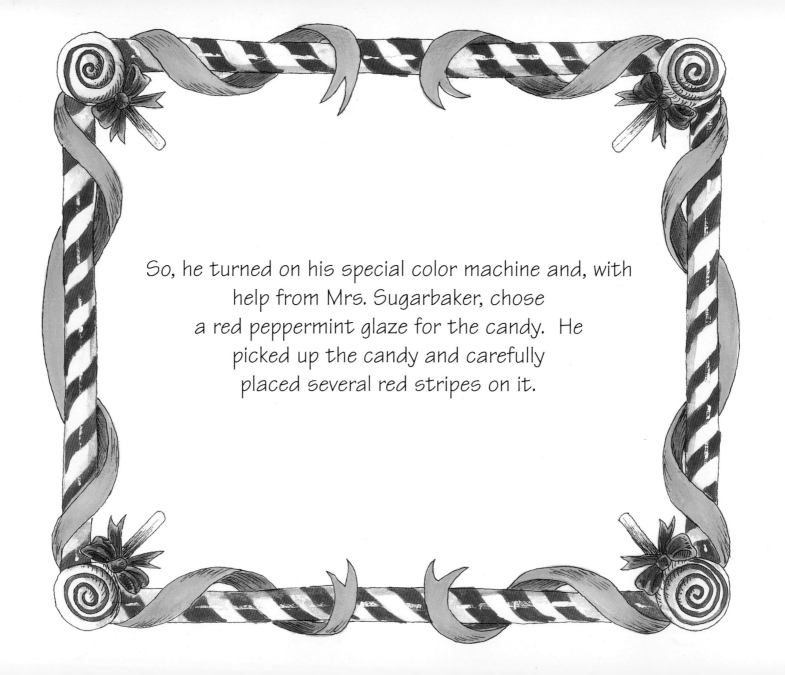

So, he turned on his special color machine and, with
help from Mrs. Sugarbaker, chose
a red peppermint glaze for the candy. He
picked up the candy and carefully
placed several red stripes on it.

While painting the candy he explained,
"The smaller stripes symbolize the road
Jesus traveled while teaching people the wonders
of God. The larger stripe will remind us that He
died on the cross to save us from our sins."

Mr. Sugarbaker, with a gleam in his eye,
smiled and hugged his wife showing her the
new Christmas candy. They immediately
began sharing the new candy with everyone.

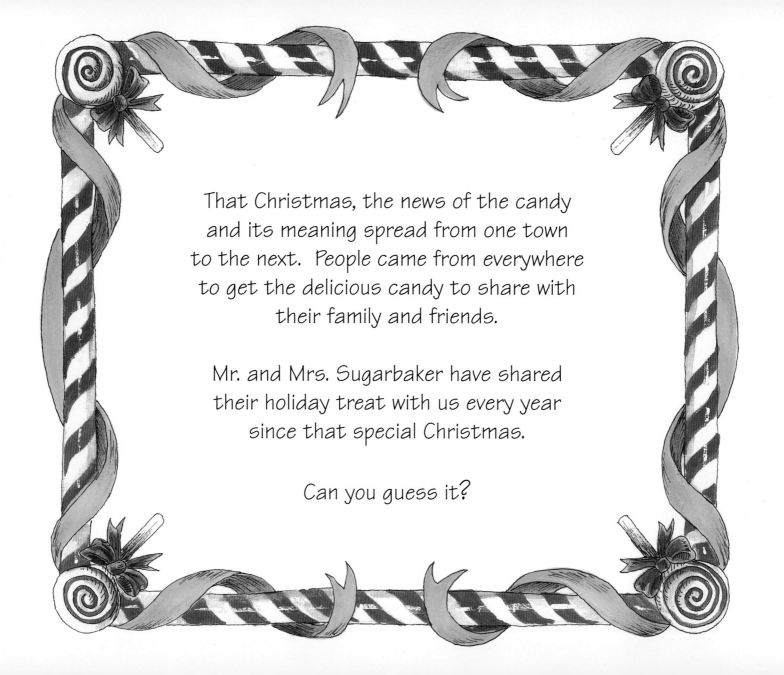

That Christmas, the news of the candy
and its meaning spread from one town
to the next. People came from everywhere
to get the delicious candy to share with
their family and friends.

Mr. and Mrs. Sugarbaker have shared
their holiday treat with us every year
since that special Christmas.

Can you guess it?

You're right. It's the candy cane!

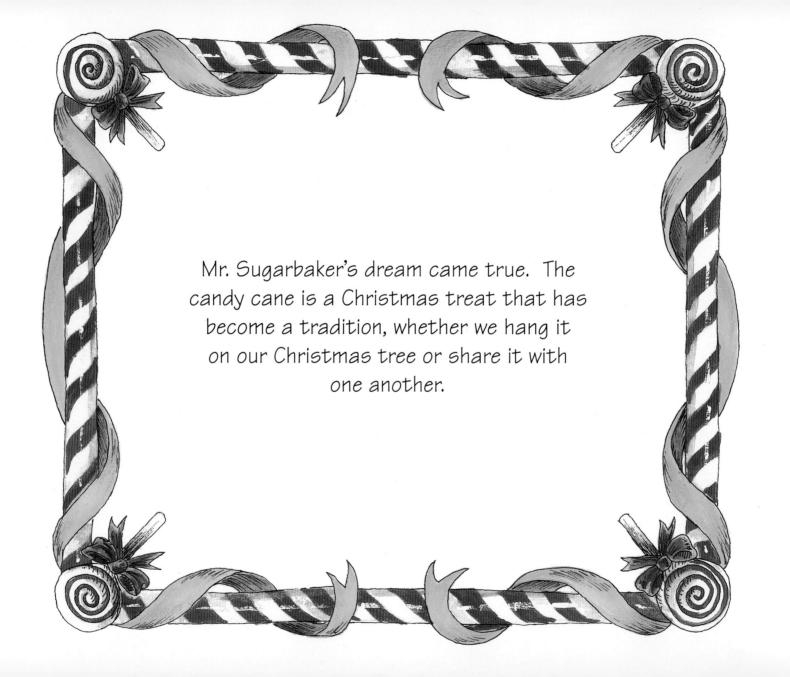

Mr. Sugarbaker's dream came true. The candy cane is a Christmas treat that has become a tradition, whether we hang it on our Christmas tree or share it with one another.

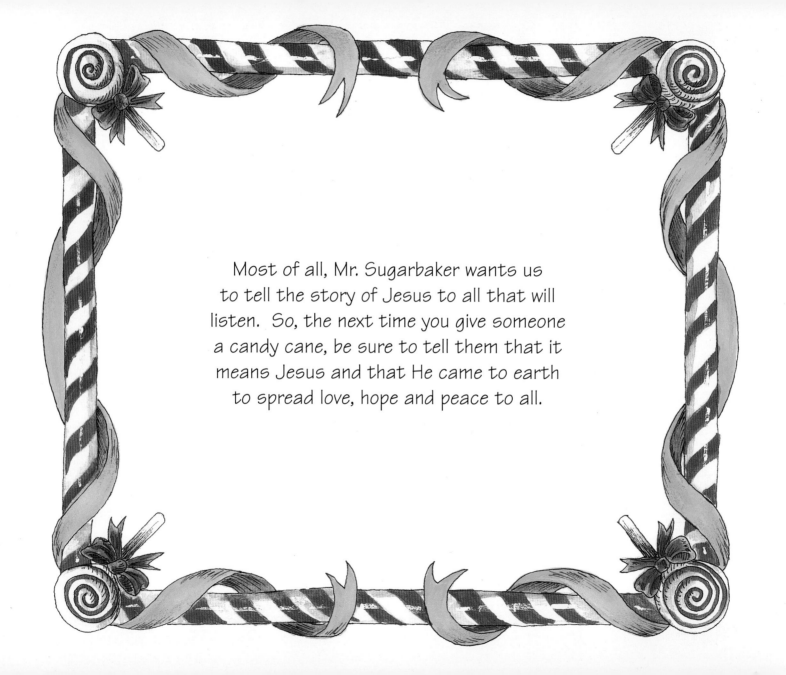

Most of all, Mr. Sugarbaker wants us
to tell the story of Jesus to all that will
listen. So, the next time you give someone
a candy cane, be sure to tell them that it
means Jesus and that He came to earth
to spread love, hope and peace to all.